W9-CVA-771

$1+1=2$

$\ldots 5 = 4-2=2$

$4+3=7$ $=6$ 8

$6-1=5$ 2

FIRST GRADE TAKES A TEST

Story by **Miriam Cohen**
Pictures by **Lillian Hoban**

Greenwillow Books
New York

Text copyright © 1980 by Miriam Cohen
Illustrations copyright © 1980 by Lillian Hoban
All rights reserved. No part of this book
may be reproduced or utilized in any form
or by any means, electronic or mechanical,
including photocopying, recording or by any
information storage and retrieval system,
without permission in writing from
the Publisher, Greenwillow Books,
a division of William Morrow & Company, Inc.,
105 Madison Avenue, New York, N.Y. 10016.

Printed in the United States of America
First Edition
10 9 8 7 6 5 4 3 2 1

Library of Congress
Cataloging in Publication Data

Cohen, Miriam.
First grade takes a test.
Summary: The first grade is distressed by an
intelligence test which fails to measure true aptitude.
[1. Examinations—Fiction. 2. School stories]
I. Hoban, Lillian. II. Title. PZ7.C6628Fi
[E] 80-10316 ISBN 0-688-80265-6
ISBN 0-688-84265-8 lib. bdg.

For Monroe who gave me the idea,
and for David who has lots of good ideas

With thanks to the North Dakota Study Group
on Evaluation—especially to Lillian Weber,
Deborah Meier, Ann Cook, and Vito Perrone

A lady from the principal's office
came to the first grade.
She had a big pile of papers with
little boxes all over them.

She smiled at the first grade.
"We have some tests for you," she said.
"Oh, good," said Anna Maria.
"Now we can find out how smart we are."

Their teacher told first grade how to do the test. She said, "Read the questions carefully. Then take your pencil and fill in the box next to the right answer.

You must work quickly.
But do not worry—
you can do it.
Ready! Begin!"

George looked at the test. It said:

Rabbits eat
☐ lettuce   ☐ dog food   ☐ sandwiches

He raised his hand.

"Rabbits have to eat carrots,
or their teeth will get too long
and stick into them," he said.
The teacher nodded and smiled,
but she put her finger to her lips.
George carefully drew in a carrot
so the test people would know.

Sammy read:

What do firemen do?

make bread ☐

put out fires ☐

sing ☐

He poked Willy. "Firemen get your head out when it's stuck," he said. "My uncle had his head stuck in a big pipe, and the firemen came and got it out."
But none of the boxes said that.

On the test there was a picture of Sally and Tom.
Sally was giving Tom something. It looked like
a baloney sandwich. Underneath it said:

Sally is taller than Tom. ☐

Tom is taller than Sally. ☐

Jim wondered what being tall had to do with getting a baloney sandwich. And was it really a *baloney* sandwich? It might be tomato. ... Jim took a long time on that one.

Suddenly the teacher said, "The time is up!"
"I'm not finished!" cried everyone except
Anna Maria. But the teacher had to take
the tests away.

Anna Maria was smiling and telling everyone,
"That was *easy.*"

"Ooh," Sara said, "I *know* I did it wrong!"
"Don't worry," Jim said. "You're as smart as I am."

One day, after they had almost forgotten the test,
the lady from the principal's office came back.
She said to Anna Maria,
"Come with me, dear."
And they went away down the hall.

When Margaret came back from getting a drink of water, she told everybody, "Anna Maria is in the special class because she did a good test!" Everyone looked around the room.

Paul was mad. He said to Danny,
"You're not going with Anna Maria, dummy!"
"You're a dummy!" Danny said.
Everybody began calling someone else
"Dummy! Dummy!"
Jim whispered it to himself. "Dummy!"

"Listen to me!" They had never
heard their teacher sound like that.
"The test doesn't tell everything.
It doesn't tell all the things
you *can* do!

You can build things! You can read books!
You can make pictures! You have good ideas!
And another thing. The test doesn't tell you
if you are a kind person who helps your friend.
Those are important things."

Everybody was quiet.
Then the teacher
brought out cookies
she had made.

When Danny got his, he yelled,
"Sara got a fatter cookie than I did!"
"Mine is fatter, but yours is wider,"
Sara said.

"Let me see!" They all looked at Sara's
and Danny's cookies and felt them.
But nobody could tell which was bigger.

Jim said, "Let's weigh them!"
They rushed to the scale.
Both cookies weighed the same!
"Good thinking, Jim!" said the teacher.

Everybody went back to work. Jim and Paul
started fixing their undersea racing car.
Sara sat in the rocker reading a good book
called *Worms: Our Friends in the Earth.*

Margaret helped George
with his arithmetic.
By the time the bell rang,
everyone felt a lot better.

Every day, Anna Maria went to the special class. But first thing each morning she peeked into first grade to tell them things. On Monday she said, "Don't forget to water the plants."

On Tuesday she asked, "Who is reminding the teacher when it is time to pass out the papers?"

On Wednesday she told Sara, "Margaret doesn't know how to help George with his arithmetic."

On Thursday she whispered something to the teacher.

And on Friday, when the first grade came
running into their room, Anna Maria
was sitting in the rocking chair.

"Aren't you in the special class anymore?"
everyone asked.

"No," said Anna Maria. "I told them I had
to come back. I told them first grade needs me."
"It's good to be together again," said the teacher.
"We don't need a test to tell us that!"

1+1=2 -5= 4-2=2

+3=7 =6 =8

6-1=5 2 =1